PETR HORÁČEK

A Best Friend for Bear

WALKER BOOKS
AND SUBSIDIARIES
LONDON • BOSTON • SYDNEY • AUCKLAND

Black Bear was feeling lonely.
I wish I had a friend,
he thought.
"But where will I find one?"

Finding a friend is not easy.

"Hello! Who's this?"
Black Bear asked himself.
"Hello," said Brown Bear,
sounding a bit surprised.

"What are you doing here?" asked Black Bear.

"I am looking for a friend," answered Brown Bear.

"What a coincidence," said Black Bear. "I am also looking for a friend! Why don't we look for a friend together?"

"That's a good idea!" agreed Brown Bear. "Let's start looking."

"Finding a friend is not easy," said Black Bear.

"No, it isn't," agreed Brown Bear.

"But it is exciting," said Black Bear.

"And easier, when there are two of us," said Brown Bear.

"Yes, because we can help each other,"
agreed Black Bear.

Brown Bear and Black Bear looked everywhere, but it was difficult to find a friend.

"Maybe we should practise with each other," said Brown Bear.

"Why don't you hide and I will try to find you?"

"Good idea,"
said Black Bear.

"Found you!" said Brown Bear.
"Now it's my turn to hide."

"Are you ready?"
shouted Black Bear.
"Coming, ready or not."

"Found you," said Black Bear.
"We're getting really good
at this."
"Yes!" agreed Brown Bear.
"Shall I hide again?"

"Ok!" said Black Bear.

This time, Black Bear couldn't find
Brown Bear anywhere.

"What if I never find him," said Black Bear.
"What if I have lost him for ever ... and ever?"

But then...

OO!

"OH! There you are!"
said Black Bear.
"On the branch!"

"I am so glad you found me!"
said Brown Bear.
"I was getting worried that I would
never find my friend," said
Black Bear, happily.

"Isn't it amazing how you can find
a friend where you least expect it?"

"On a branch, you mean?" asked Black Bear.

And they both laughed.

To Norah and Ebbe with love

First published 2022 by Walker Books Ltd, 87 Vauxhall Walk, London SE11 5HJ

2 4 6 8 10 9 7 5 3 1

© 2022 Petr Horáček

The right of Petr Horáček to be identified as author/illustrator of this work has been
asserted by him in accordance with the Copyright, Designs and Patents Act 1988.

This book has been typeset in WB Horáček

Printed in China

British Library Cataloguing in Publication Data: a catalogue record for
this book is available from the British Library

ISBN 978-1-4063-9754-3

www.walker.co.uk